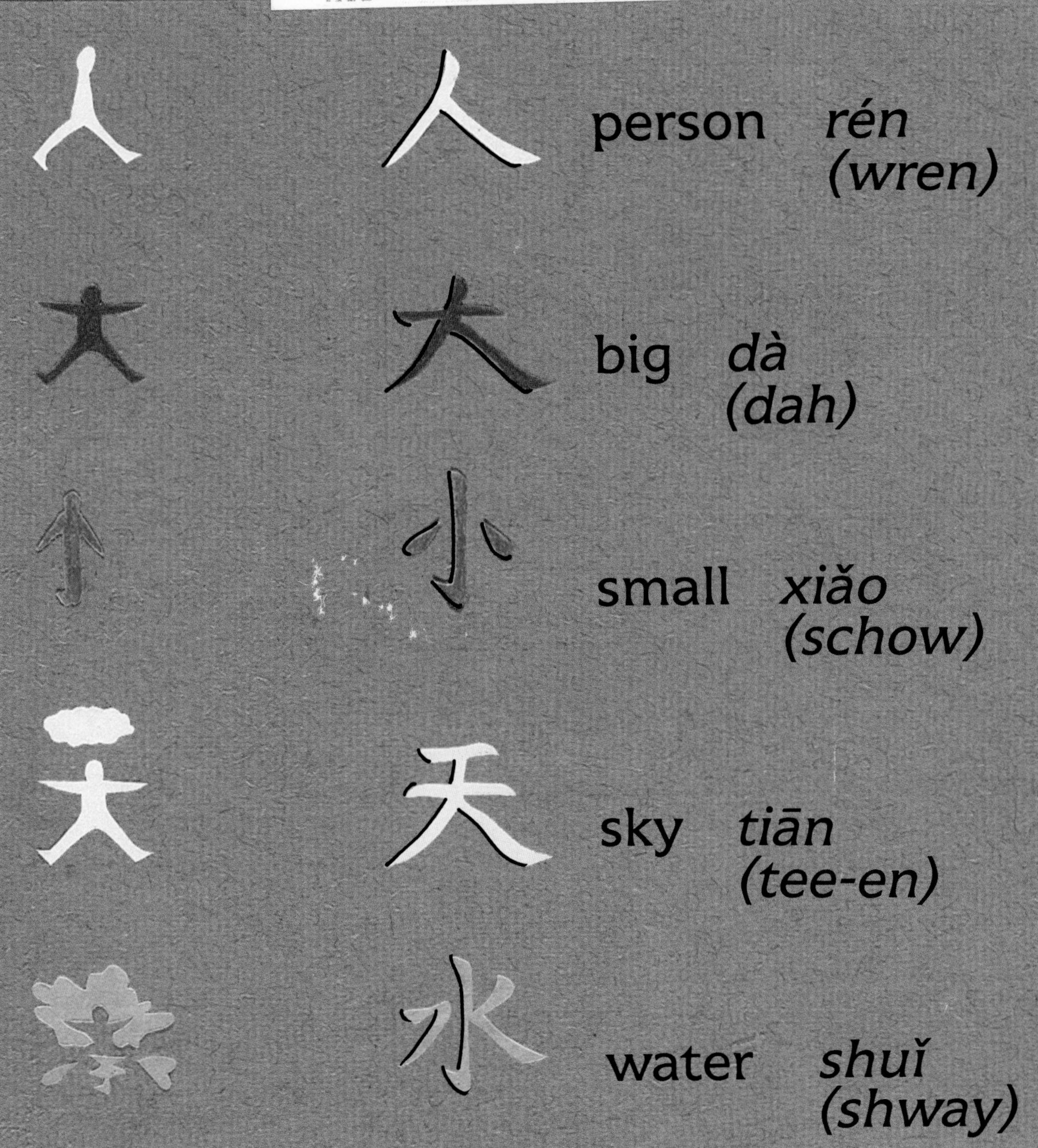

Pronunciation of words in parentheses are approximations of Mandarin Chinese.

Henry Holt and Company, Inc., *Publishers since 1866*
115 West 18th Street, New York, New York 10011
Henry Holt is a registered
trademark of Henry Holt and Company, Inc.

Published in Canada by Fitzhenry & Whiteside Ltd.,
195 Allstate Parkway, Markham, Ontario L3R 4T8.

Library of Congress Cataloging-in-Publication Data
Lee, Huy Voun.
At the beach / written and illustrated by Huy Voun Lee.
Summary: A mother amuses her young son at the beach by drawing in the sand Chinese characters, many of which resemble the objects they stand for.
1. Chinese language—Writing—Juvenile literature.
[1. Chinese language—Writing.]
PL1171.L33 1994 495.1'82421—dc20 93-25462

ISBN 0-8050-2768-8 First Edition—1994
Printed in the United States of America
on acid-free paper. ∞
10 9 8 7 6 5 4 3 2 1

For my mother

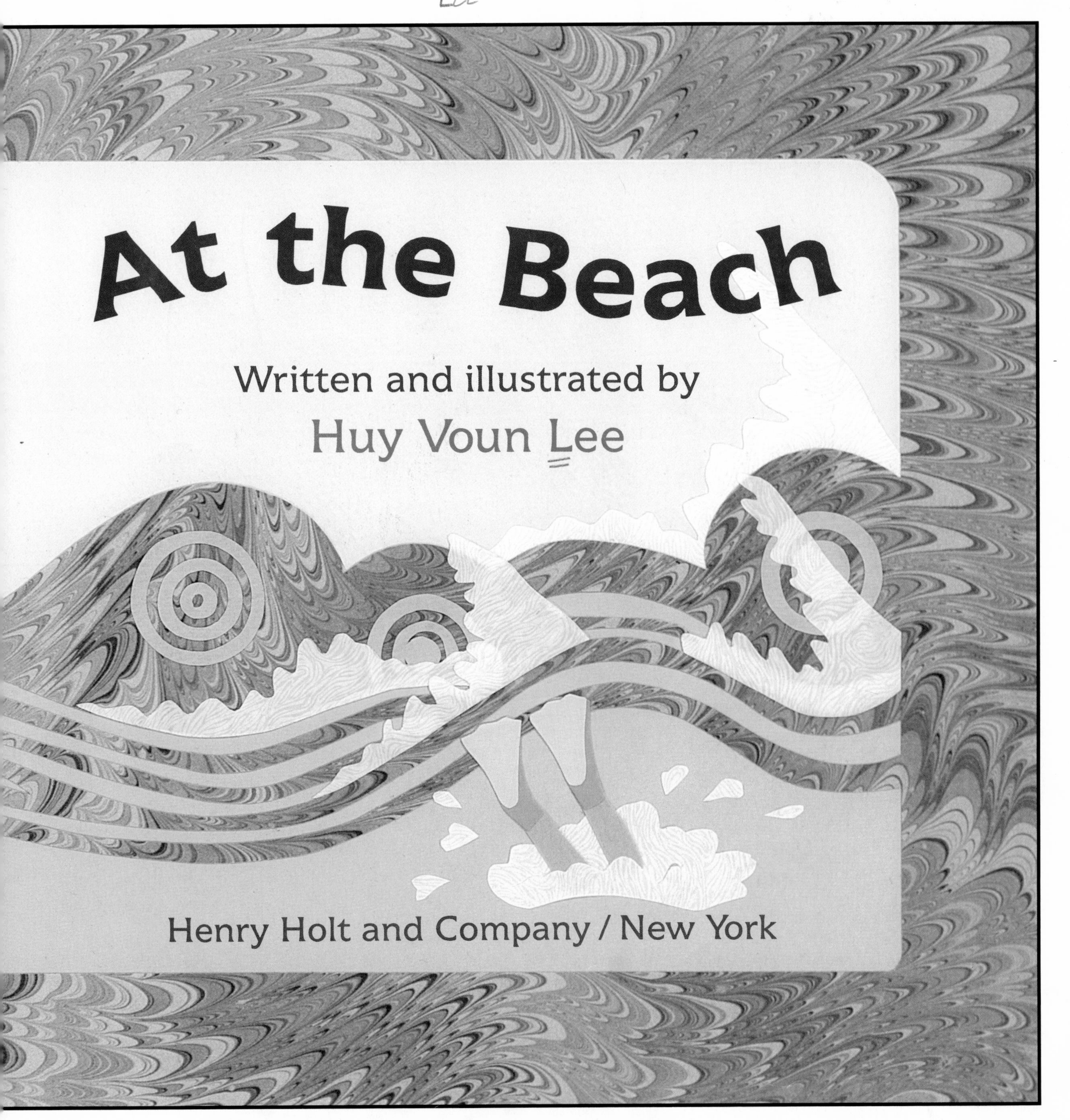

At the Beach

Written and illustrated by

Huy Voun Lee

Henry Holt and Company / New York

It is a beautiful day at the beach.

Xiao Ming is learning to write Chinese.

"Many Chinese characters are like pictures," says his mother as she draws in the sand.

人 "I know that character," says Xiao Ming. "It means *person*. See, it looks like someone walking."

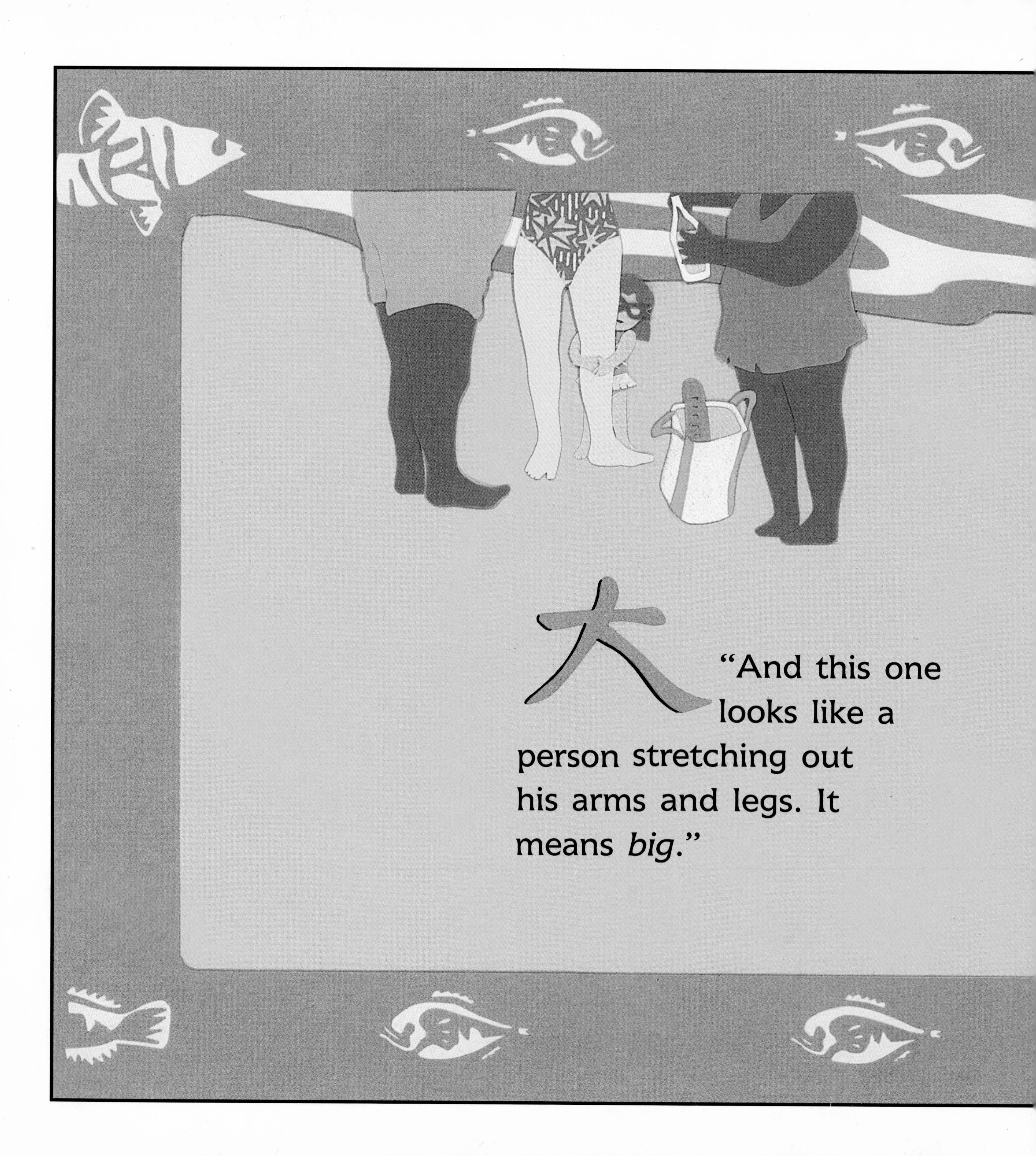

大 "And this one looks like a person stretching out his arms and legs. It means *big*."

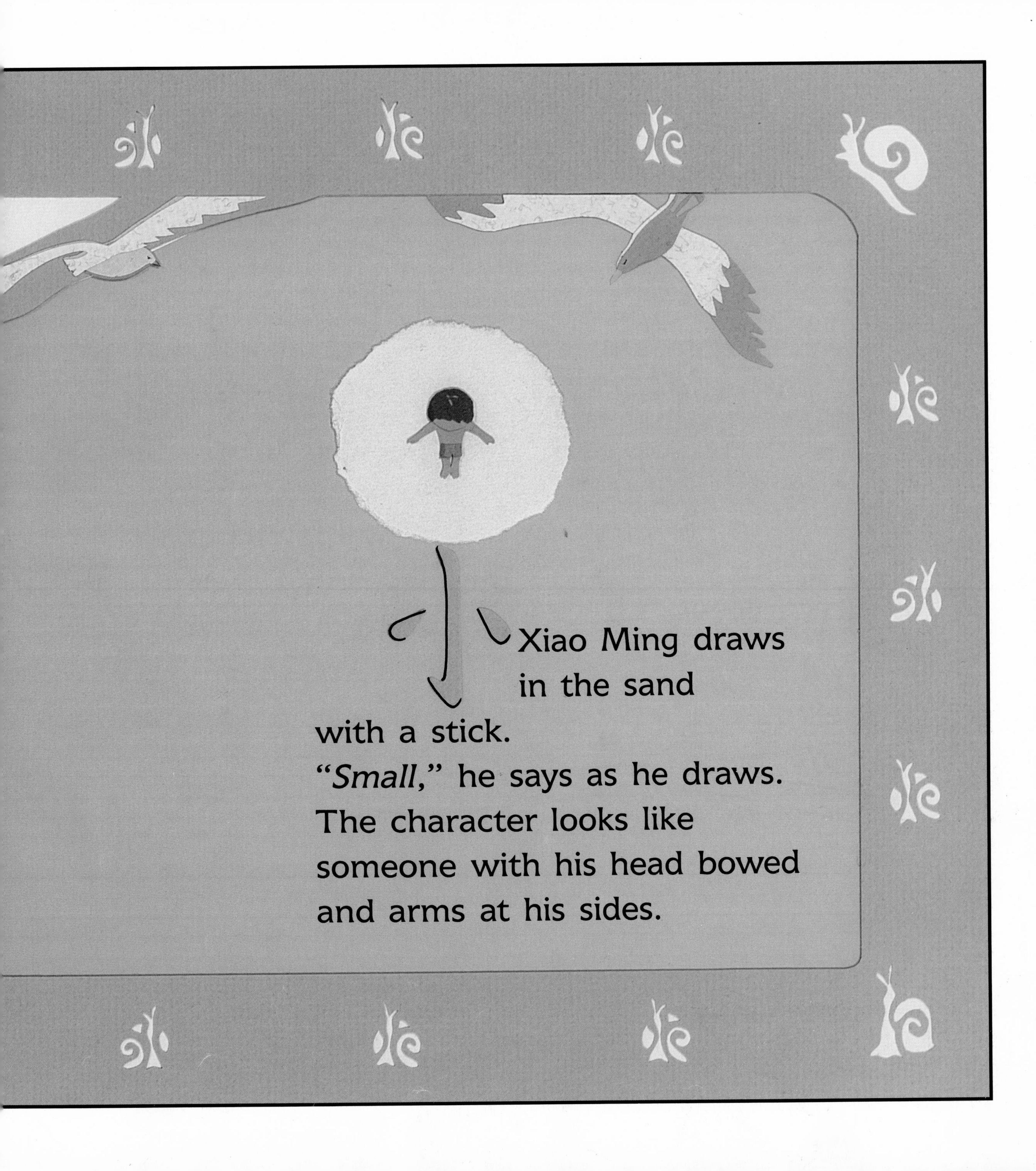

Xiao Ming draws
in the sand
with a stick.
"*Small,*" he says as he draws.
The character looks like
someone with his head bowed
and arms at his sides.

"Do you remember the character for *sky*?" his mother asks. "First you draw the character for *person* and then you put a line above."

水 "I know what *water* looks like," Xiao Ming says. "A big splash!"

山 “And *mountain*
is easy to remember,”
says his mother,
“because the character
looks like a group of
three mountains.”

沙 "But *sand* needs a little more imagination. First, because sand is found near the water, there are three strokes symbolizing water. Can you help me draw them?" she asks as she continues. "Next comes the character for *small*. . . ."

"Because grains of sand are small!" Xiao Ming adds.

That's right," says his mother. "And finally, there's
 long stroke at the bottom as if someone were
igging in the sand."

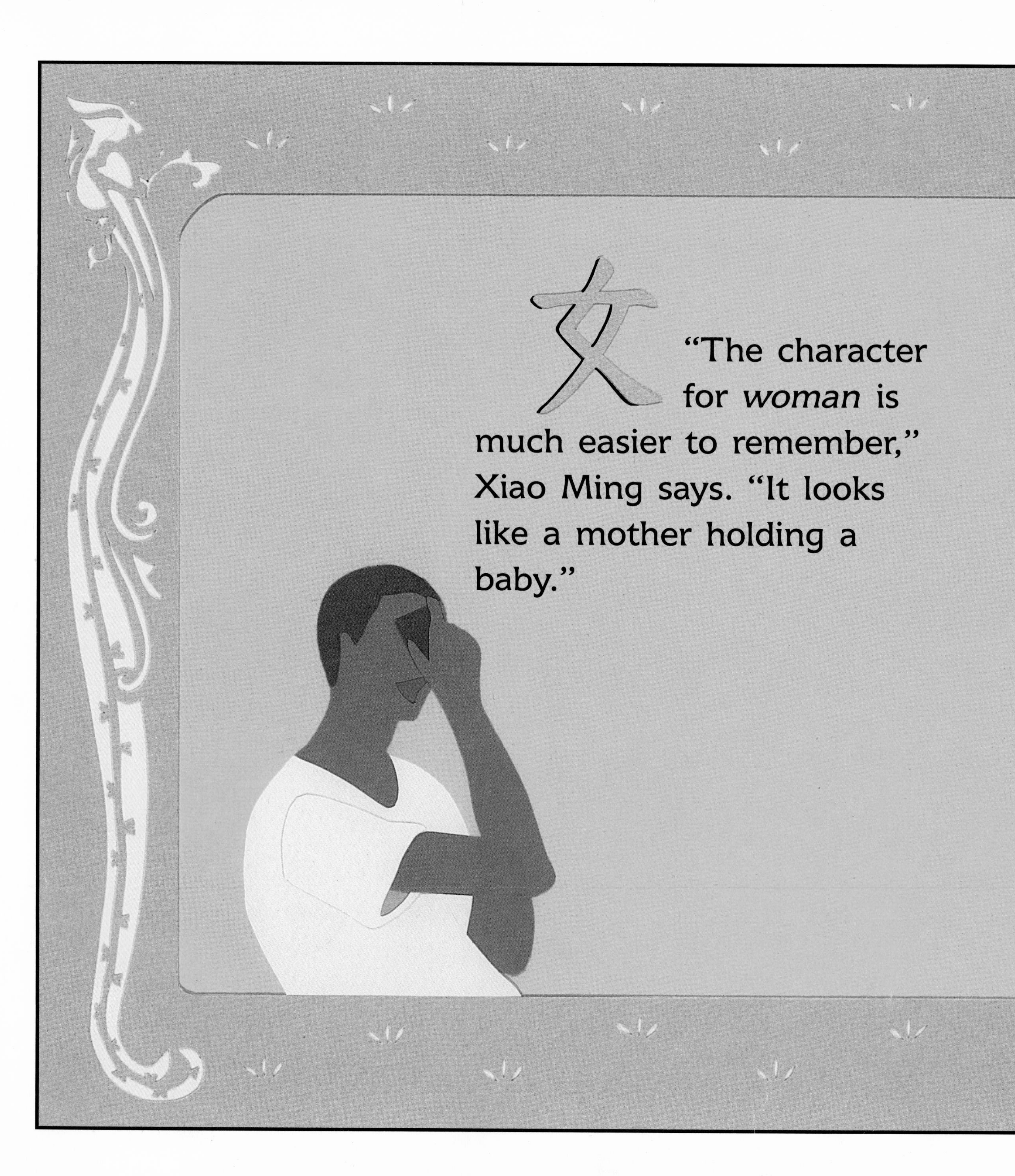

女 "The character for *woman* is much easier to remember," Xiao Ming says. "It looks like a mother holding a baby."

子 "And the character for *child* is easy too, because it looks like a child serving his parents."

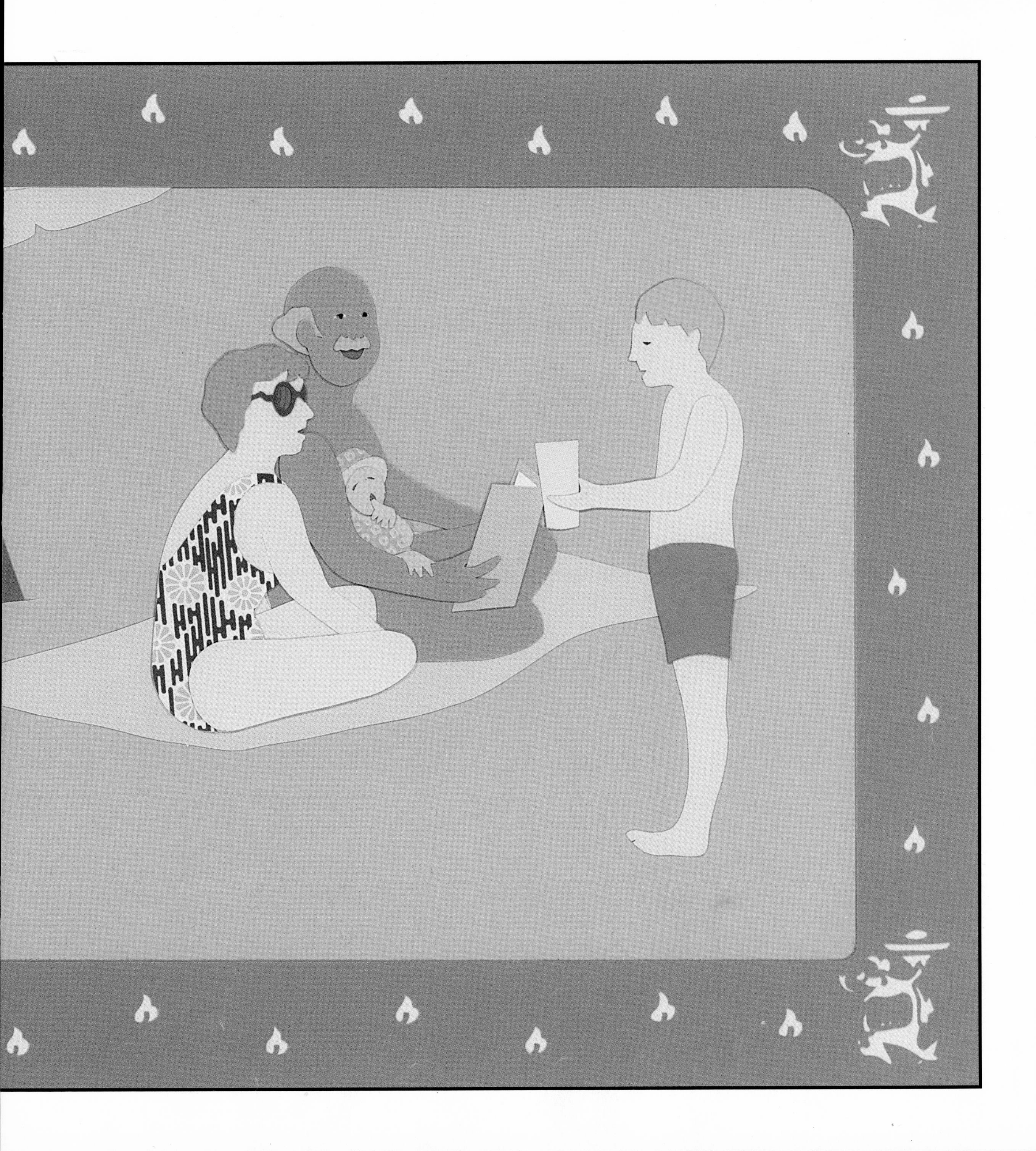

好 "What word do you make when you put *woman* and *child* together?" asks his mother.

"Good," says Xiao Ming. Then he smiles. It has been a good day at the beach.

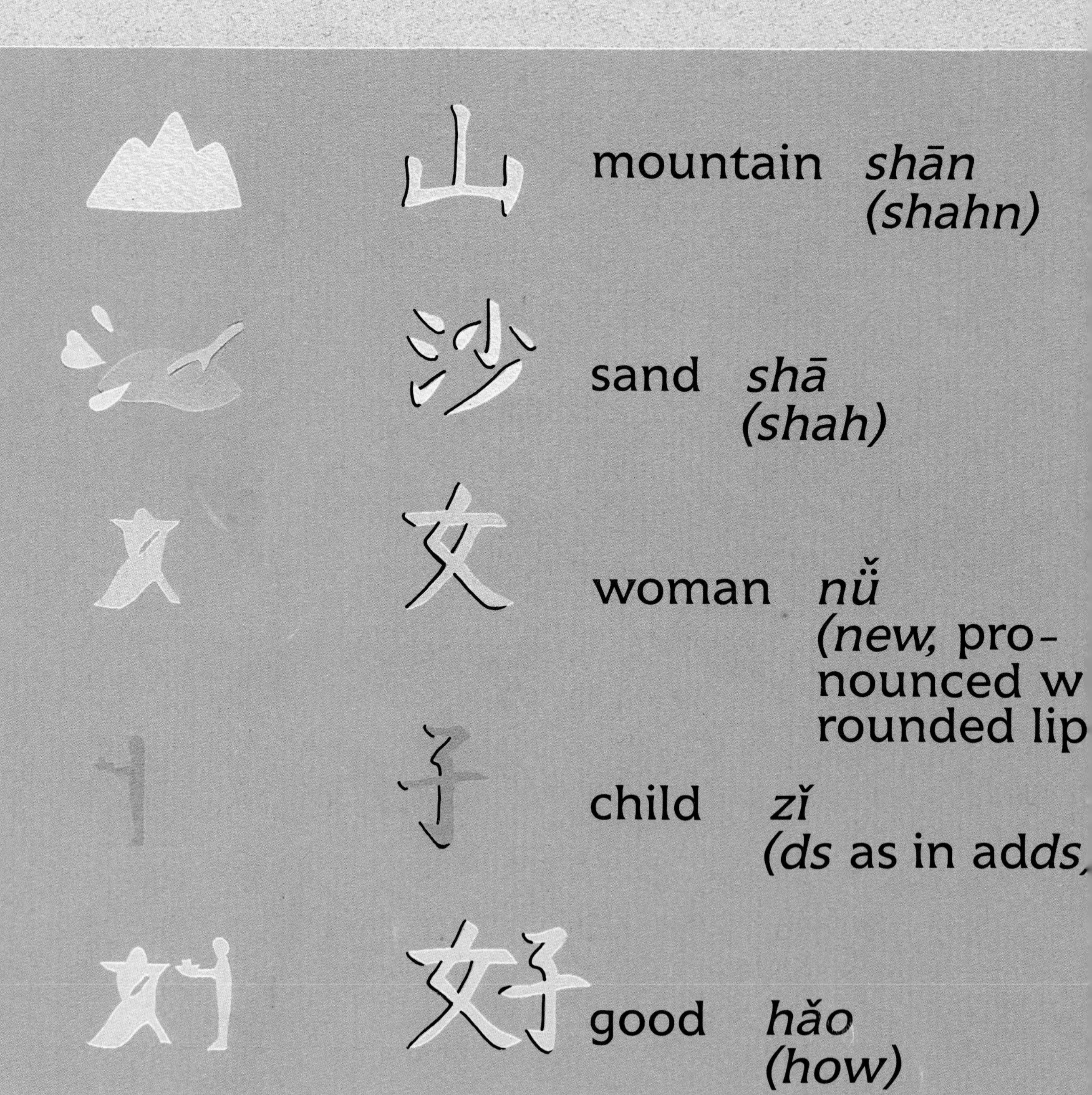
山
mountain shān
(shahn)
沙
sand shā
(shah)
女
woman nǚ
(new, pro-
nounced w
rounded lip
子
child zǐ
(ds as in adds,
好
good hǎo
(how)